For Rosie—of course, and Polly too.

J. H.

For Audrey Keri-Nagy and her little Rose.

H. C.

First U.S. edition 2002

Library of Congress Cataloging-in-Publication Data

Hindley, Judy.
Rosy's visitors / by Judy Hindley ; illustrated by Helen Craig. —1st U.S. ed.
p. cm.
Summary: Rosy transforms a tree trunk into her own house for the day, where she entertains imaginary friends.
ISBN 0-7636-1769-5
[1. Dwellings — Fiction. 2. Imagination — Fiction. 3. Hospitality — Fiction.] I. Craig, Helen, ill. II. Title.
PZ7.H5696 Ro 2002
[E] — dc21 2001037892

2 4 6 8 10 9 7 5 3 1

Printed in Italy

This book was typeset in Poliphilus MT.
The illustrations were done in colored pencil and watercolor.

Candlewick Press
2067 Massachusetts Avenue
Cambridge, Massachusetts 02140

visit us at www.candlewick.com

Rosy's Visitors

Judy Hindley

illustrated by Helen Craig

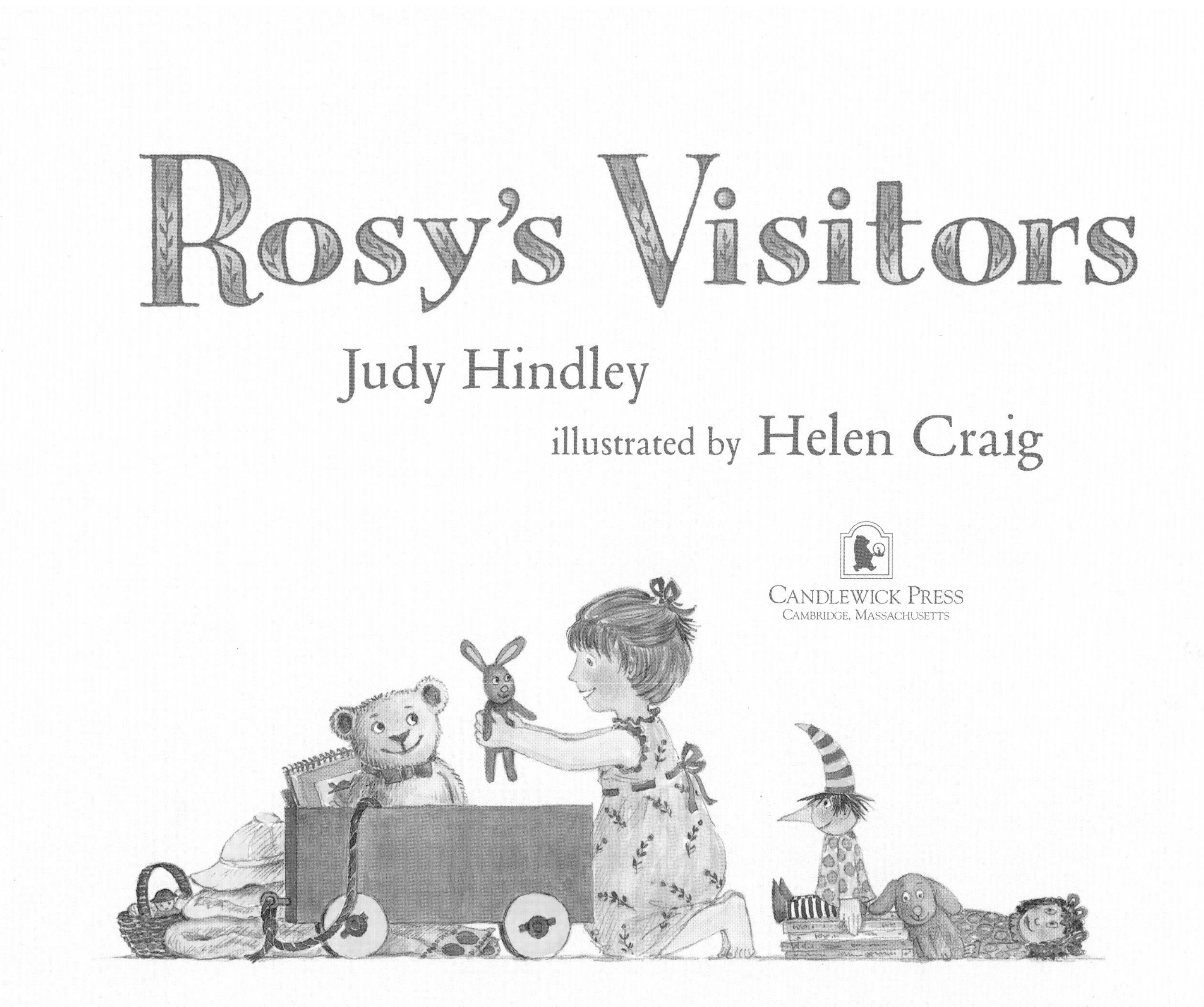

CANDLEWICK PRESS
CAMBRIDGE, MASSACHUSETTS

One day Rosy said,
"Today is moving day.
I'm going to find myself
a whole new house."
She packed up her blanket
and her pillow, and her
books and toys, and
all her favorite things . . .
and started looking.

Very soon she found a little house.
She peeked in through the door.
She looked all around.
"This is it! This is my house!"
cried Rosy. "What a
perfect house."

Rosy got busy.
"This is my house; it's mine,
all mine!" she sang.
She swept and
cleaned her
house, and
made it neat.

She hung up her coat and
rain hat, and she made her bed.
She found a special place to
sit and think, or draw,
or read her book.

When she was finished,
Rosy clapped her hands.
"This is my house;
it's Rosy's house!"
she sang.
And she put up a sign
so everyone could
see that this was
Rosy's house.

"Hmm," said Rosy. "I wonder if visitors will find my house. I think I need a path so visitors can find the way."

She found some stones and things, and marked a path right up to her front door.

Then she said, “Now I
need a bell for visitors to ring.”
She found a jingle bell and
hung it by the door.
“There!” she said. “Now
everything is perfect. I’m
ready for visitors. I wonder
if anyone will come.”

Rosy took her spyglass
and looked out the window.
With her spyglass
she could see far, far away.
She could see far across the
land and out over the sea,
and way up high,
high into the sky.

ROSY'S
HOUSE

And there they were.
There were Rosy's visitors, coming in
from the sea, and down from the sky,
and all across the land . . .
to Rosy's house.

"Welcome to my house!" cried Rosy.
Rosy's visitors came up the path
and rang the bell, and said hello.
They bowed and curtsied, and they
all brought gifts because
it was their first visit.

Then
they came
in the house and
tried out everything.
They all loved Rosy's house.
They had a tremendous feast,
and they sang and they danced . . .

ROSY'S HOUSE

till they were so tired out they had to leave.

"Goodbye! Goodbye!" they called.

"Come again!" cried Rosy.

Rabbit

When they had gone,
Rosy had lots of
cleaning up to do.
Then she packed up
her things, looked
through her spyglass
one last time . . .

and went back home,

and she was just in time for supper.